Bunnies on Ice

Johanna Wright

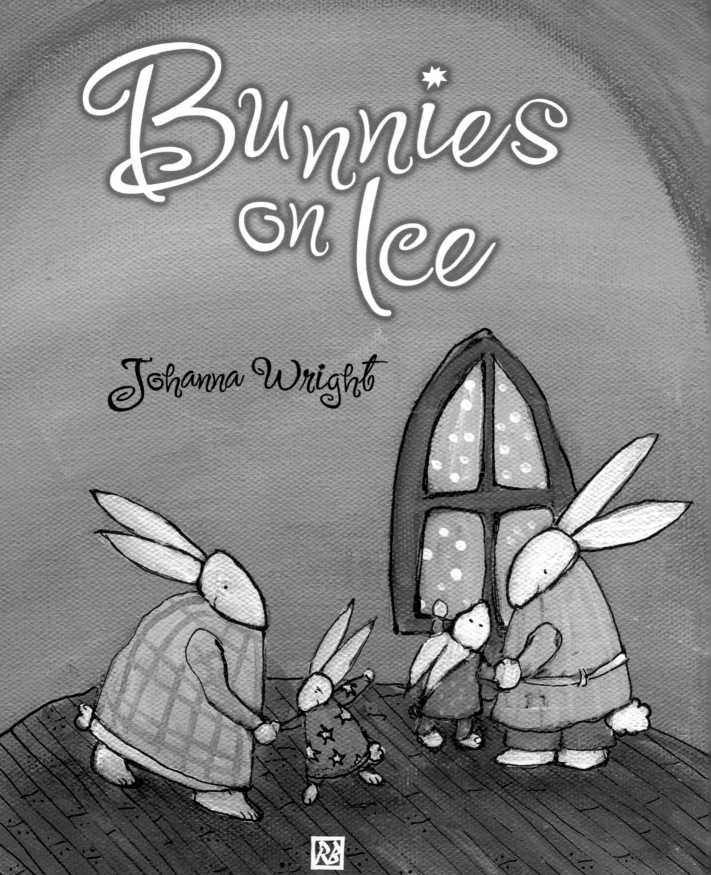

A NEAL PORTER BOOK
ROARING BROOK PRESS
NEW YORK

Copyright © 2013 by Johanna Wright

A Neal Porter Book

Published by Roaring Brook Press

Roaring Brook Press is a division of Holtzbrinck Publishing Holdings Limited Partnership

175 Fifth Avenue, New York, New York 10010

mackids.com

Library of Congress Cataloging-in-Publication Data

Wright, Johanna.

Bunnies on Ice / Johanna Wright. — 1st ed.

p. cm.

"A Neal Porter Book."

Summary: A confident and determined young rabbit demonstrates how to be
a champion ice-skater.

ISBN 978-1-59643-404-2 (hardcover)

[1. Ice skating—Fiction. 2. Self-confidence.—Fiction. 3.
Rabbits—Fiction.] I. Title.

PZ7.W9496Bun 2013

[E]—dc23

2012001187

Roaring Brook Press books are available for special promotions and premiums.
For details contact: Director of Special Markets, Holtzbrinck Publishers.

First edition 2013

Book design by Jennifer Browne and Roberta Pressel

Printed in China by South China Printing Co. Ltd., Dongguan City, Guangdong Province

1 3 5 7 9 10 8 6 4 2

For Gabe

The best thing about my family
is that we're really good at ice-skating,
but I am a champion.

When you're a champion ice-skater, you have to wait for the conditions to be just right.

And wait . . .

And wait . . .

Until . . .

. . . it's time!

I tell my Dad, "I have to eat
a very big breakfast because
I am a champion ice-skater."

I say, "When you are a champion
ice-skater, you have to wear a
LOT of clothes."

But not too many.

I have a lot of fans.

I can spin faster than anyone.

I can do a figure
eight with my
eyes closed.

I can leap into the air and land perfectly
every time, just like a champion ice-skater.

Well, almost.

When you are a champion ice-skater, it's very important to have an excellent support team . . .

and drink plenty of hot chocolate . . .

and eat a balanced diet . . .

and keep your muscles loose.

Get some rest . . .

and try again tomorrow.